SHINING

JULIUS LESTER

ILLUSTRATED BY JOHN CLAPP

SILVER WHISTLE • HARCOURT, INC.

ORLANDO   AUSTIN   NEW YORK   SAN DIEGO   TORONTO   LONDON

For Paula, who shines
—J. L.

For Mary, my sun and my moon
—J. C.

Text copyright © 2003 by Julius Lester
Illustrations copyright © 2003 by John Clapp

www.HarcourtBooks.com

Silver Whistle is a trademark of Harcourt, Inc., registered in the United States of America and/or other jurisdictions.

Library of Congress Cataloging-in-Publication Data
Lester, Julius.
Shining/Julius Lester; illustrated by John Clapp.
p. cm.
"Silver Whistle."
Summary: A young girl who has not uttered a sound since birth is shunned by the people in her village, until they realize how special she is.
[1. Mutism, Elective—Fiction. 2. Africa—Fiction.] I. Clapp, John, ill. II. Title.
PZ7.L5629Sh 2003
[E]—dc20 95-48904
ISBN 0-15-200773-3

C E G H F D B

Printed in Singapore

The art for this book was created using graphite, charcoal, chalk, and pastels;
watercolor, gouache, and acrylic paint, on Arches hot- and cold-press watercolor papers, and Strathmore hot-press bristol board.
The display type and text type were set in Adobe Jensen.
Color separations by Bright Arts Ltd., Hong Kong
Printed and bound by Tien Wah Press, Singapore
This book was printed on totally chlorine-free Enso Stora Matte paper.
Production supervision by Sandra Grebenar and Pascha Gerlinger
Designed by Linda Lockowitz

Author's Note

The primary passion of my childhood and adolescence was music, so much so that until the last week of my college career, I thought I was going to be a musician. I played classical piano for a number of years as well as guitar and banjo, and was a professional folksinger during my twenties.

Because of my musical beginnings I think musically when I write. The sounds and rhythms of sentences are as important to me as the cognitive meanings conveyed. Sentences must flow from one to another as effortlessly as a line of music unfolds logically from note to note.

Just as a composer or jazz musician will set out to create variations around a musical theme or in a particular key, *Shining* is a set of variations around the theme of the color black. I wanted to create figures of speech in which the color black would be associated with goodness and beauty rather than evil and ugliness.

One of the joys of being a writer at this time in history is having the opportunity to create new stories to offset the old stories in which blacks (among many others) are portrayed as something less than or other than what we are—human. Given how deeply embedded in our culture are negative associations to the color black, many stories will be required before a balance is achieved.

Shining is one attempt at creating the new stories blacks and whites need. However, *Shining* is also a coming-of-age story about the journey of a soul who learns that our most important connection to others may not be in talking but in listening.

Any resemblance between the people portrayed here and the blacks of Africa is purely coincidental. Shining is a wholly imaginative creation which came to me one winter day as I was driving somewhere, and the image came to me so powerfully that I pulled off the road, found a piece of paper in the glove compartment, and scribbled down the opening lines of the story before they escaped me.

Finally, my family will tell you that I have a fanatical need of and passion for silence and that I listen far more than I talk. Anyone who sees Shining as part of the author's autobiography would not be guilty of misreading.

—J. L.

Illustrator's Note

I see my task as a book illustrator as creating visuals that echo the story, eliciting emotion in harmony with the text. As I research a book and gather reference materials over several months, certain sources will resonate—a passage in a piece of music, the way an artist represented a face in an ancient painting; these cumulative impressions help shape the book's aesthetic. The work of painter Alphonse Mucha, Chinese paintings of the Lingnan School, and African sculptures have all found their way into *Shining* over the past two years.

This book was unusual: timeless and archetypal, a large story—larger than specific places or cultures. In creating the art for *Shining*, I was searching for imagery that defied dating, and depictions of faces that speak more about humanity than specific cultures. I wanted the faces to communicate a broader idea of a person, or a goddess, without calling to mind a familiar face. The stricter realism of my other books seemed inappropriate. I hope that, in the end, we have created a book for all ages, cultures, and perspectives.

—J. C.

ONCE UPON A TIME and long, long ago, in a mountain village far, far away, a girl as black and silent as wonder was born.

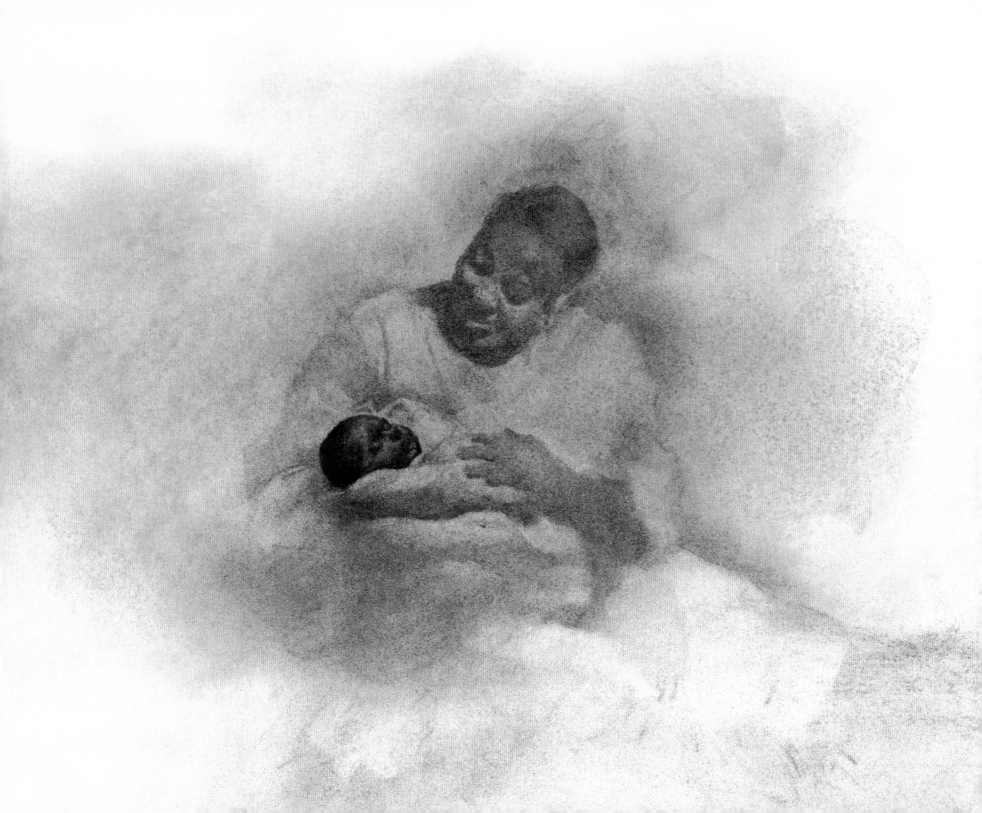

"I do not hear my baby," Solgi, the mother, called out.

Nya, the old midwife, was worried, too. The child did not cry with surprise when her nakedness was bathed with cool water. She made no sounds of pleasure as Nya wrapped her in a warm, soft cloth and placed the child in her mother's arms.

Solgi looked at her daughter. The child was black as wisdom and stared back with a gaze as bottomless as the unknown. "She looks at me as if she knows what has been and what will be."

Nya managed a smile as weak as a cool breeze on a hot day. "This world will cause her to cry out soon enough. But your husband waits for word of his child."

Nya went outside and beckoned to the tall man sitting a distance away.

"Is something wrong?" Kimaru asked, hurrying to the midwife. "I did not hear any birth cries."

"You have a healthy daughter" was all Nya could say.

A smile as wide as kindness opened on his face when he looked at his child. "Solgi, she is so black her skin shines bright like the sun."

And that is how she came to be called Shining.

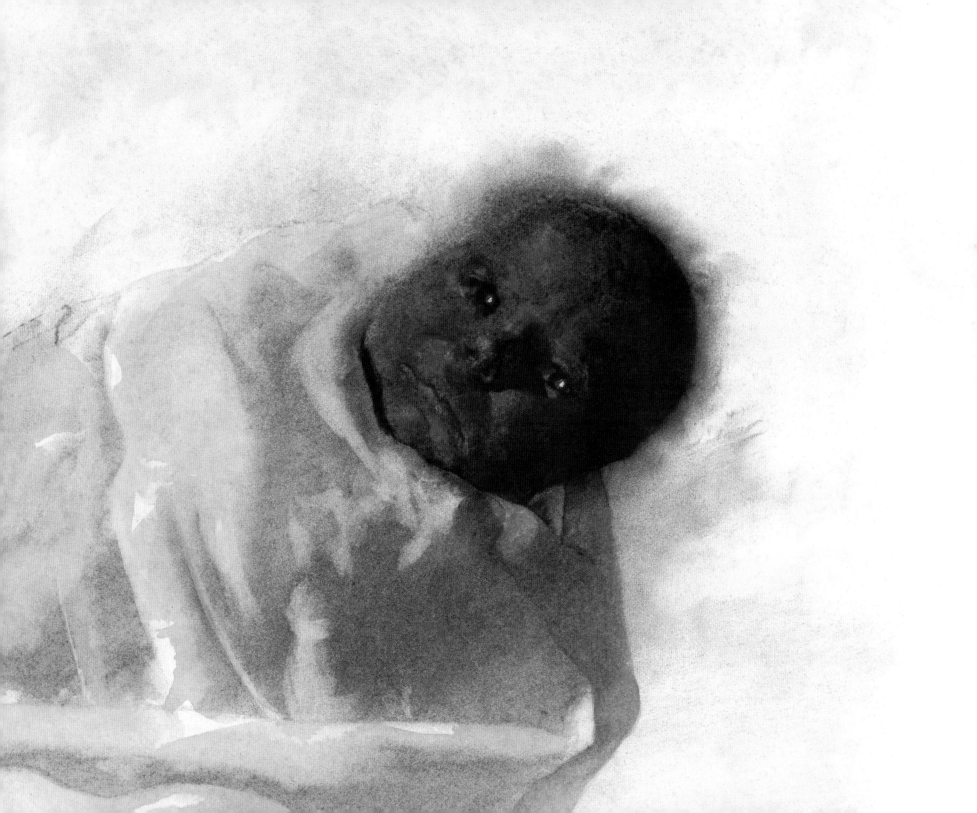

"Why is she so quiet? Is she deaf?" Kimaru asked the midwife anxiously.

"I do not think so," Nya answered.

"You do not *think* so?" the father exclaimed. "I need to *know*!"

Without warning he clapped his large hands loudly next to one of the baby's ears. The child shuddered like Sky at the sound of Thunder. Tears as dense as sorrow poured from her eyes, but she made no sound.

Seeing his child's silent pain, Kimaru said, "I am sorry." He took the child from his wife. "I did not mean to hurt you. Please forgive me," he whispered as he looked into Shining's face.

Kimaru saw that she not only heard but understood his words. Frightened, he handed the child back to his wife and fled outside. Nya was frightened, too, of this child who made no sound when she was in pain.

Shining grew. When she played, she did not cry aloud when she fell, though glistening tears flowed down her black face. No laughter tumbled from her belly when she was happy, though her face was as bright as dawn. Such silence made children and adults uneasy, and they did not want to be around her.

Shining could have spoken or laughed or cried aloud at any moment. She knew she was not supposed to, but she didn't know why.

Kimaru was suspicious of her silence. "She can talk," he insisted. "But all she does
is listen."

"What should we do?" Solgi asked.

"Take her to The One. She will know."

The next morning, as Sun flamed Mountain awake, Solgi put Shining in a sling and followed a trail up into the hills. Parrots and monkeys chattered and screamed as they passed. Shining listened as if hearing her own voice.

The path narrowed as it went deeper into the forest. Suddenly the cool shadows turned into a warm darkness that shone like a snake's hypnotic gaze.

"Release the child," a voice as husky as evening commanded.

Solgi saw only blackness. If she could have seen the path, she would have turned and run away.

"Release the child." A woman sheathed in a robe as red as the dying sun appeared, and light rushed in like water. She was taller than fear and as black as the earth after a rainstorm. *The One.* She guarded and tended the souls of the living and the dead. If anyone would know what was wrong with Shining, she would.

"Release the child," The One repeated, coming closer.

Solgi put her daughter down.

Without hesitation, Shining ran to The One, as if meeting her true mother. The One, arms wide, stooped and hugged her.

Solgi's heart ached like an egg about to burst as she saw Shining embrace The One as she had never embraced her mother.

"Why do you come here?" The One asked Solgi.

"My daughter is two and she does not talk. She has never even made a sound. I fear an evil spirit has taken her voice."

"Your husband fears that there is evil in Shining. There is no more than in him or you—or me," The One said simply.

"You—you know her name?"

"And much more."

"Then tell me. I am her mother. Why doesn't she talk and cry and laugh? It is not natural."

"For her it is." The One pulled Shining closer and whispered, "I will meet you on the other side of Silence."

"What did you say to her?" Solgi demanded to know.

The One said nothing as she gave Shining back to her mother. Tears ran down the girl's face as she reached out for The One to take her back. The One smiled. Shining understood and she relaxed into her mother's arms.

Shining's black silence seemed
to extend roots into the black
earth, and the child grew tall like
a prayer soon to be answered.

The adults and children of the
village saw, and Shining's silence
frightened them even more.

Time passed. On the morning
she became twelve, her mother
took her to a stream, and there
bathed her face.

"Today you begin preparation
for The Parting. At the next New
Moon, you and the other girls
who have reached this time will
be taken to the sacred compound
in the mountains. There, all of
you will live for a year and Nya
and the Council of Women will
teach you the ways of women."

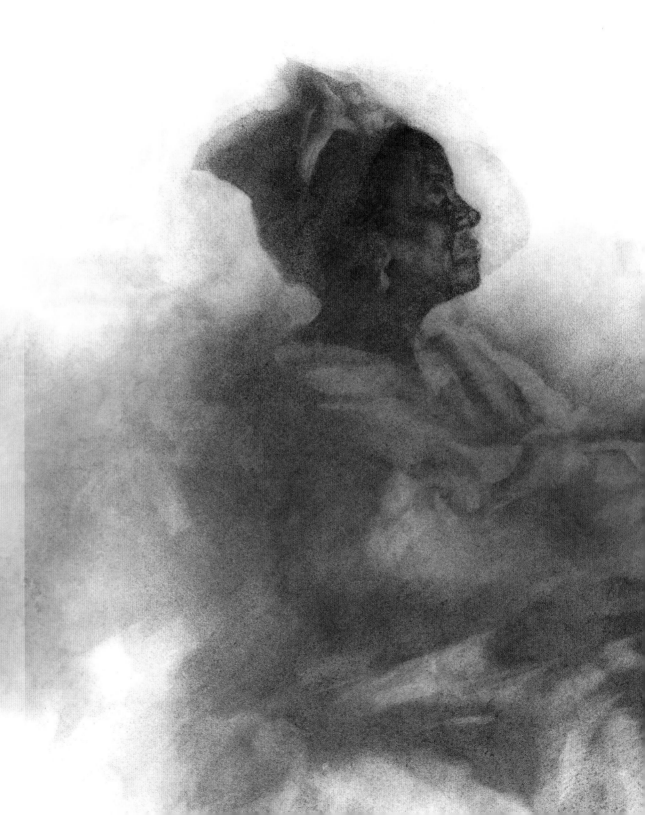

At last, Shining thought, the time had arrived when she would reach the other side and her silence end.

"I will teach you to sew your ritual robes just as my mother taught me, just as you will teach your daughters," her mother told her.

The Day of the New Moon arrived. Shining dressed in the blue ritual robe she had sewn with her mother. With her parents beside her, she walked to the center of the village where the other girls robed in noon blue waited with their parents.

When she entered the clearing, all talking stopped. Shining went to join the other girls. The girls moved back. Shining stopped, her heart pounding so hard she feared she would die.

Nya and the Council of Women entered the clearing, and saw the girls huddled together, as if for protection against the black child standing alone like the last shining star. Nya frowned.

She went to Shining and, speaking softly, said, "There is no kind way to put this. You cannot go for The Parting. Since the night you were born, you have not made a sound. I know you can. A child who can speak and refuses to do so must be evil. We cannot allow you to live among us. Your silence steals people's souls."

As her parents screamed, Shining slumped to the ground, as if killed by a knife as sharp as a lie.

Weeping, Kimaru picked up his daughter and carried her back to the hut. She was not dead but neither did she live. Moon went from sliver to full and back again, over and over, until a year passed. Shining had not awakened.

Then came the morning when the sound of singing was heard far away. Mothers and fathers awoke and hurried to the center of the village to see the flames of torches bobbing down the mountainside as those who had left as girls returned as women. Wearing the sun yellow robes of adulthood, they danced into the village to the sound of drums.

At first no one, except Solgi, noticed the woman as tall and black as destiny who strode into the village looking neither right nor left. Her robe was as red as Time and flowed behind her like ribboned Wind. On her head an oval basket was balanced. As people became aware of her, the drumming slowed and then stopped. The dancing came to a halt. People backed away from her in fear. Then, there was only silence.

It was The One! She had never come into the village. She set the basket on the ground and her eyes searched every face, as if seeking one in particular. Not finding it, she stretched forward her long, dark arms. "Come, my daughter!" she called out.

Everyone looked around. Whom was she speaking to? "Look!" someone shouted.

From the far end of the village, Shining walked toward them wearing a robe as yellow as noon—her black skin shining like jewels. The crowd parted, and Shining walked toward The One. Everyone gasped when they saw how much alike the two looked.

The One opened her arms and Shining stepped inside. The One's embrace was like a cloak no wind would ever go through. The One looked at her and Shining heard. She had arrived at the other side of Silence.

Shining could speak now. But what would she say? She did not know. Then she smiled. Silence knew.

Shining opened her mouth. A wordless song as soft as blackness came out of the Silence. But no one had ever heard music such as this. It was made from the screeches of monkeys, the calls of birds, and the growls of leopards. The people listened and heard water crashing against rocks and leaves trembling in the wind. The people listened more closely, and there was the sound of this one crying and that one laughing. Those who listened closest of all heard the sound of their hearts when they were most afraid.

Finally, Shining stopped. Silence had become a language. It told the people that Shining had heard all their joys and all their sorrows and, especially, their fears. It told the people that she was there to listen, especially to that which they could not hear.

The One took from her basket a robe flowing red like love. "This is The One who will be," she announced, placing the robe on Shining.

The people came forward, dropped to their knees, and bowed until their heads touched the earth.

"Forgive us," Shining heard them say, though their mouths had not opened.

And she forgave.

Shining hugged her mother and her father and Nya, who had brought her into the world.

Then Shining and The One walked from the village and went to that place high
in the mountains where the blackness, shining like silence, burned against the stars.